retu

For Tom and the moles on Marden Hill

First published in Great Britain in 1995
by Orion Children's Books
a division of the Orion Publishing Group Ltd
Orion House
5 Upper St Martin's Lane
London WC2H 9EA

A catalogue record for this book is available from the British Library

Typeset by Deltatype Ltd, Ellesmere Port, Cheshire.
Printed in Italy

ISBN 1 85881 133 3

Murdoch Mole's
Big Idea

Georgie Adams

Illustrated by Chris Fisher

Orion
Children's Books

The oak tree, which had stood for over two hundred years, blew down on Monday morning.

Bert watched the tree fall.
"I'm impressed," he said.
"Did I do that?" said Murdoch Mole.
"Saw it with my own eyes," said Bert. "One minute you were tunnelling. Next thing, *whoosh!* The tree fell down."
"Wow!" said Murdoch.

On Tuesday Murdoch was in the vegetable garden looking for worms. He was peering under some cabbages when he thought he saw one. It was the biggest worm he had ever seen.

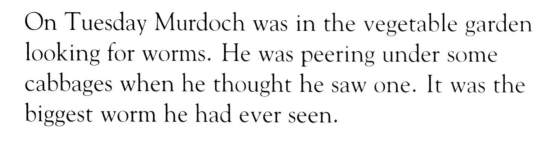

But when Murdoch grabbed it for lunch, a jet of water shot into the air.

"Brilliant! A bird-bath," said Bert.
"Did I do that?" said Murdoch.
"There it is," replied Bert, "and full of birds already!"

On Wednesday Murdoch dug a new
tunnel. It went around the oak tree . . .

beyond the vegetable patch and . . .

under the wall . . .

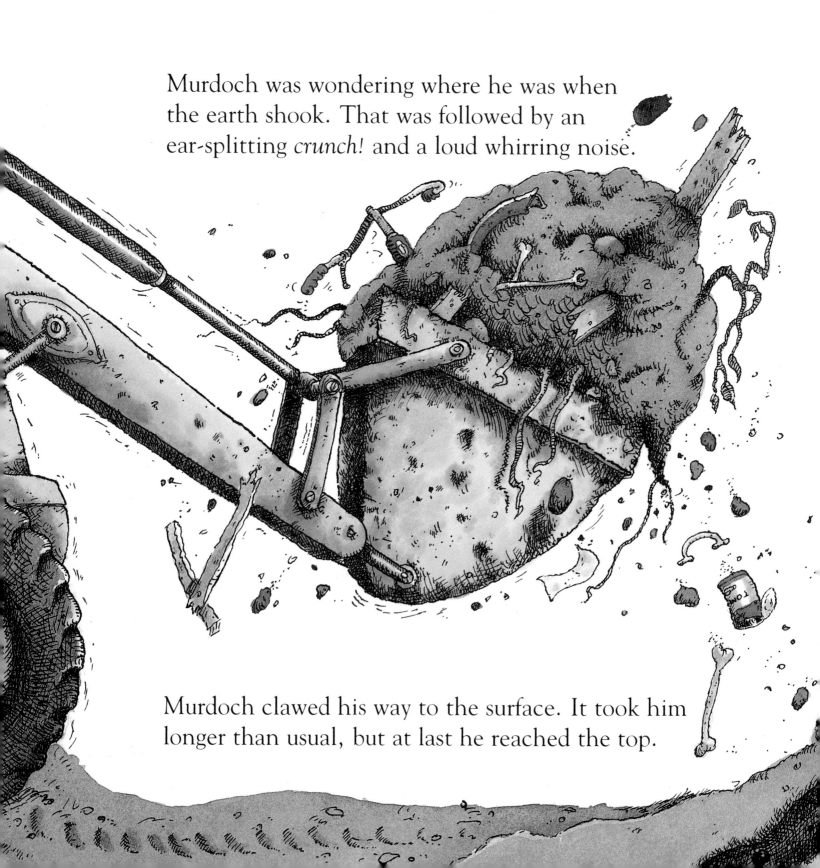

Murdoch was wondering where he was when the earth shook. That was followed by an ear-splitting *crunch!* and a loud whirring noise.

Murdoch clawed his way to the surface. It took him longer than usual, but at last he reached the top.

"Amazing!" said Bert. "The biggest molehill in the world."
"Did I do that?" said Murdoch, looking down from a great height.
"All by yourself," said Bert with a grin.
And Murdoch swelled with pride.

At home that evening, Murdoch sat in his favourite chair.

He thought about the tree, and the bird-bath. He thought about the molehill – the biggest molehill in the world!

And that gave Murdoch an idea.
A BIG IDEA.

Murdoch would turn his molehill
into a tourist attraction.
It would be famous!

On Thursday morning Murdoch found some chalk and a piece of wood and made a noticeboard.

Then he set off. No doubt there would be some early visitors to the molehill and Murdoch was eager to show them around.

There was no one waiting for him.
In fact, Murdoch couldn't see anything at all.
He looked carefully to make sure he was in the
right place. He was. But the biggest molehill in the
world had disappeared.

Murdoch thought of his big idea.
There was no time to lose.
He would have to start again.

Murdoch worked hard all day. From time to time he popped his head above the ground to have a look, but his molehill was no bigger than, well . . . a molehill.

Owl, who had been watching, flew down.
"What *are* you doing?" she asked.
"Making the biggest molehill in the world," replied Murdoch,
"or rather, *another* one."
And he told Owl what had happened.

"Oh dear!" interrupted Owl. "I'm afraid a bulldozer did all that. It was clearing the ground for a new road. It must have cleared away your 'molehill' too."

Murdoch looked dismayed.

"Bert said I made it," he said, "and I believed him."

"Bert would," said Owl crossly. "It was his idea
of fun."

Murdoch felt useless. A nobody. Just a very ordinary
mole with silly big ideas.

As they were talking, a duck came along.

"There is *something* you could do," said Duck. "Something you do very well."

"What's that?" said Murdoch gloomily.

"Dig a tunnel," said Duck.

"Why would *you* need a tunnel, Duck?" said Murdoch.

"*I* don't," said Duck. "But I know someone who does."

Duck waddled off and came back with . . .

. . . a toad!
The toad looked upset.
"I can't get home," she said. "My pond is on the
other side of the new road."
"Which is where the tunnel comes in," explained Duck.
"Leave this to me," said Murdoch.

Murdoch disappeared underground while Owl, Duck,
the toad and some friends waited patiently on top.
Murdoch dug all through Friday and Saturday.
By Sunday the job was done.

Murdoch's Tunnel (as it was to be known) went right under the new road. Thanks to Murdoch, toads and other small creatures could cross safely from one side of the road to the other.

Everyone cheered. Murdoch was exhausted, but happy.
He felt he had done something Really Useful. He was
wanted after all. He was a *somebody*.

Bert came to see what all the fuss was about.
"Did you do that?" said Bert.
"All by myself!" said Murdoch proudly.
"You're a genius!" said Bert.
"Thank you," said Murdoch.

And because something deep down inside
told him that Bert really meant it . . .
Murdoch believed him!